Notes to Parents and Teachers:

At this level of reading, your child will rely less on the pattern of the words in the book and more on reading strategies to figure out the words in the story.

REMEMBER: PRAISE IS A GREAT MOTIVATOR!

Here are some praise points for beginning readers:

- You matched your finger to each word that you read!
- I like the way you used the picture to help you figure out that word.
- I noticed that you saw some sight words you knew how to read!

Book Ends for the Reader!

Here are some reminders before reading the text:

- Use picture clues to help figure out words.

- Get your mouth ready to say the first sound in a word and then stretch out the word by saying the sounds all the way through the word.

- Skip a word you do not know, and read the rest of a sentence to see what word would make sense in that sentence.

- Use sight words to help you figure out other words in the sentence.

Words to Know Before You Read

churros

Colosseum

fries

international food festival

parade

pizza

steak

tacos

EATING Around the WORLD

By Craig Marks
Illustrated by Isabella Grott

Rourke
Educational Media
rourkeeducationalmedia.com

It is an international food festival.

Ross and Dave are excited.

Wow, the parade is awesome!

This food is from America.

Let's have steak and fries.

I want cheesecake for dessert.

Come here! It's Italy.

Yes, there's the Colosseum!

Let's have pizza.

I want gelato for dessert.

Where are we now?

We are in Mexico.
Let's eat some more!

Let's have tacos
and nachos.

I want churros for dessert.

I ate too much! I am so full.

I am full, too. I can't eat anymore.

Do you want to try this?

No more food for us!

Book Ends for the Reader

I know...

1. Why are Ross and Dave excited?

2. How did they know it was America?

3. Where can you find the Colosseum?

I think ...

1. Have you ever been to a food festival?

2. Have you ever tried Italian food?

3. Do you like trying new food?
   Why or why not?

Book Ends for the Reader

What happened in this book?

Look at each picture and talk about what happened in the story.

About the Author

Craig Marks loves to fish, boat, and enjoy the warm Florida sun. Born and raised there, he enjoyed a teaching career for many years focusing on marine science and native wildlife. With a hands-on approach, he would often bring live ocean creatures or other animals into his classroom. He loves to write on all subjects as long as he brings a smile to whoever is reading it!

About the Illustrator

Isabella was born in 1985 in Rovereto, a small town in northern Italy. As a child she loved to draw, as well as play outside with Perla, her beautiful German Shepherd. She studied at Nemo Academy of Digital Arts in the city of Florence, where she currently lives with her cat, Miss Marple. Isabella also has other strong passions: traveling, watching movies and reading - a lot!

Library of Congress PCN Data

Eating Around the World / Craig Marks

ISBN 978-1-68342-729-2 (hard cover)(alk. paper)
ISBN 978-1-68342-781-0 (soft cover)
ISBN 978-1-68342-833-6 (e-Book)
Library of Congress Control Number: 2017935444

Rourke Educational Media
Printed in the United States of America, North Mankato, Minnesota

Edited by: Debra Ankiel
Art direction and layout by: Rhea Magaro-Wallace
Cover and interior Illustrations by: Isabella Grott